FAR OUT
FAIRY TALES

raintree

THE WARRIOR VAMPIRE

THE QUEEN VAMPIRE

THE HUNTER VAMPIRE

Raintree is an imprint of Capstone Global Library Limited, a company incorporated in England and Wales having its registered office at 264 Banbury Road, Oxford, OX2 7DY – Registered company number: 6695582

www.raintree.co.uk
myorders@raintree.co.uk

Text © Capstone Global Library Limited 2017
The moral rights of the proprietor have been asserted.

Designed by Hilary Wacholz
Edited by Abby Huff
Original illustrations © Capstone 2017
Illustrated by C.S. Jennings
Lettering by Jaymes Reed

ISBN 978 1 4747 2804 1
20 19 18 17 16
10 9 8 7 6 5 4 3 2 1

British Library Cataloguing in Publication Data: a full catalogue record for this book is available from the British Library.

Printed and bound in China.

FAR OUT FAIRY TALES

GOLDILOCKS
AND THE THREE
VAMPIRES

A GRAPHIC NOVEL

BY LAURIE S. SUTTON
ILLUSTRATED BY C.S. JENNINGS

Legends say that deep within this megalithic tomb lies treasure hidden by King Arthur himself. Tomb raiders and thieves have tried to get inside. But *I'm* not here to steal.

The National Museum wants to study the tomb. That's why they called the best crypt cracker in the biz...

GOLDILOCKS
ADVENTURER EXTRAORDINAIRE

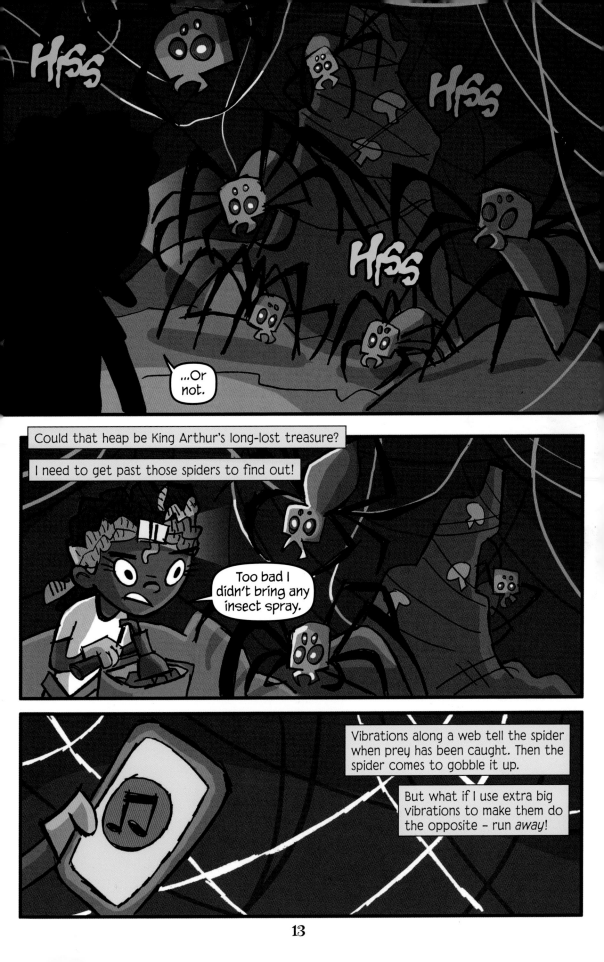

18

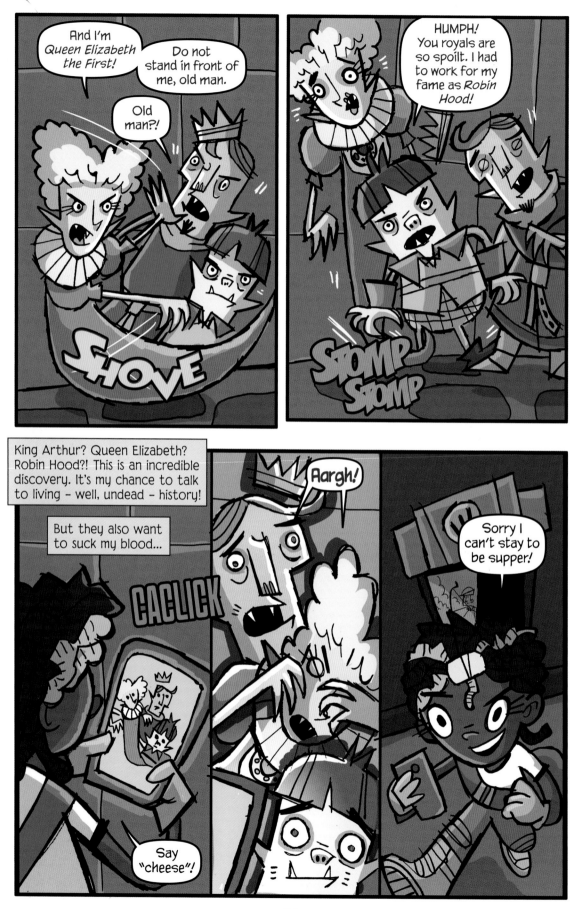

24

POP

WOOSH

FWUMP

OOF!

I'll have your golden locks as a trophy when I get out of this.

Oh yeah?

Because it looks as if *I'm* queen of this crypt.

THUMP!

FWOOSH

Curses!

ALL ABOUT THE ORIGINAL TALE!

There aren't any world-famous crypt crackers in the original tale, but in Robert Southey's 1837 version, called "The Story of the Three Bears", there is a nosy home intruder!

A little bear, a middle-sized bear and a big bear live in a house in the woods. One morning, the bears make porridge for breakfast. They decide to go for a walk to give the food time to cool.

Not long after, an old woman comes to the house. She walks in and sees three bowls of porridge on a table. She tries the porridge from the big bowl - it's too hot. Next she eats from the medium bowl - it's too cold. Finally she eats from the little bowl - it's neither too hot nor too cold, but just right. So she gobbles it up!

The woman tries out the bears' chairs. Only Little Bear's chair is just right, and she sits in it until it breaks. Then the woman lies in the bears' beds. Once again, only Little Bear's is just right. She falls asleep straight away.

The three bears come back for breakfast, only to discover someone's been eating their porridge! They also notice someone's been sitting in their chairs and sleeping in their beds. Little Bear looks at his bed and says, "Someone's been sleeping in my bed - and here she is!"

Little Bear's voice wakes the old woman. She hops out of bed and jumps out of an open window never to be seen again.

Later versions of the tale replace the old woman with a young girl who's playing in the woods. She finds the empty house and decides to explore. The little girl was called Silverhair and Goldenlocks before she was finally called Goldilocks in 1904.

In the original tale, Goldilocks just wanders into someone's house (how rude!). In this version, she's there to study the tomb and its artefacts.

Three bears have been replaced with three blood-sucking vampires!

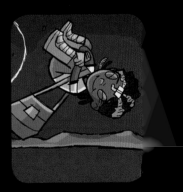

Instead of eating porridge, or trying out chairs and beds, Goldi uses her skills to avoid three tricky traps!

The original Goldilocks is woken up from a nap and runs away. In this tale, she uses her brains to escape and is ready for more adventure!

VISUAL QUESTIONS

1

Foreshadowing is when an author leaves hints about something that will happen later in the story. What is being foreshadowed here? What is causing the vampire to come out?

2

What is Goldi about to do at the end of the story? What kind of new creatures might she run into on her next adventure?

3

But I have a feeling this next adventure is going to be a lot warmer!

In your own words, describe what's happening in these two panels. Look at page 10 if you need help.

Goldi threatens to use the flash on her phone and is able to escape. But what does the reader know that the vampires don't?

Do you think the vampires are really who they say they are? Why or why not? Write a paragraph about your answer.

AUTHOR

Laurie S. Sutton has been reading comics since she was a kid. She grew up to become an editor for Marvel Comics, DC Comics, Starblaze and Tekno Comix. She has written *Adam Strange* for DC, *Star Trek: Voyager* for Marvel, plus *Star Trek: Deep Space Nine* and *Witch Hunter* for Malibu Comics. There are long boxes of comics in her wardrobe where there should be clothes and shoes. Laurie has lived all over the world but currently resides in Florida, USA.

ILLUSTRATOR

C.S. Jennings loves to draw. He takes his sketchbook and drawing tools wherever he goes. As a freelance illustrator, he draws lots of stuff, e.g. for video games, board games and books (like this one!).

GLOSSARY

artefacts objects made and used by humans long ago

constellation group of stars that forms a shape, such as an object, animal or person

crypt underground room, often used as a burial place for the dead (or undead)

document make note of something through writing, photography or film to prove that it happened or existed

extraordinaire extremely skilled at something

megalithic a megalith is a very large stone used by ancient cultures as part of a building or as a monument. If something is megalithic, it is similar in looks to a megalith.

portrait picture of a person's face and shoulders, often painted or drawn

raiders people who enter a place to steal. A tomb raider breaks into tombs in order to steal valuables buried with the dead.

spelunking activity of exploring caves. A spelunking shirt is a shirt designed specially for the exploration of caves.

tomb grave, room or building for holding dead bodies

transform change a great deal, such as in your actions or appearance

vibrations fast movement back and forth

AWESOMELY EVER AFTER.